STAR STRIKER TITCH

Little Titch wants to play a big part in the school
World Cup – if only he could get on the pitch!

Martin Waddell has written many books for children,
including the picture books *Farmer Duck* and *Can't
You Sleep, Little Bear?*, both of which have won the
Smarties Book Prize. Among his many fiction titles are
Cup Final Kid, Cup Run, Going Up! and *Shooting Star*,
and in 2004 he was awarded the prestigious Hans
Christian Andersen Award for services to children's
literature. Martin lives with his wife Rosaleen in
Newcastle, County Down, Northern Ireland.

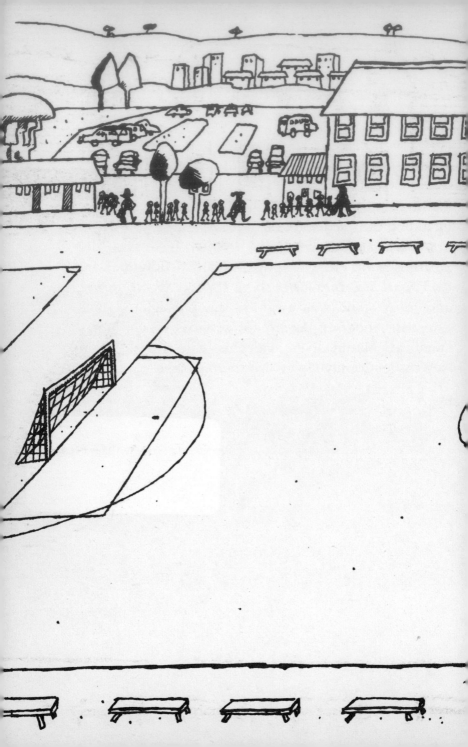

Books by the same author

Cup Final Kid

Cup Run

Ernie and the Fishface Gang

Going Up!

MARTIN WADDELL

Star Striker
Titch

Illustrations by Russell Ayto

WALKER
BOOKS

For Donard FC
Newcastle Co. Down
M.W.

First published 2003 by Walker Books Ltd
87 Vauxhall Walk, London SE11 5HJ

This edition published 2005

4 6 8 10 9 7 5 3

This book has been typeset in Garamond

Printed in Great Britain by J.H. Haynes & Co. Ltd

British Library Cataloguing in Publication Data:
a catalogue record for this book
is available from the British Library

ISBN-13: 978-1-84428-969-1
ISBN-10: 1-84428-969-9

www.walkerbooks.co.uk

Contents

Chapter One
9

Chapter Two
14

Chapter Three
23

Chapter Four
31

Chapter Five
36

Chapter Six
46

BUNGO'S TEAM

"It is the school five-a-side World Cup Day for our year, and we're going to win it!" said Bungo. "I'm calling us Bungo's Team."

"It's a *World* Cup," Ravi said. "We should be named after a country."

"It's *my* team!" shouted Bungo. "I choose the name!"

There were seven squad players for each team to pick from. That was five in the team, and two subs, so everyone would get a game, even the tinies like Titch and Cosmo.

Bungo picked himself first. Then he picked Dunky and Ravi and Leroy. That made four, but it was *five*-a-side.

"Tony *must* be in the team," Ravi said. "He's the best player we have."

"Tony will have to play to *my* orders!" Bungo said. "I'm the biggest. That makes me king of this team!"

Bungo's Team lined up for their
first World Cup match. The game
was played on the five-a-side pitch
at school, with the five-a-side goals,
and Mrs Pearl's five-a-side rules.

"TEAM SCHEME!" announced
Bungo. "Leroy in goal. Tony and
Ravi at the back. Dunky feeds me
from the middle. I'm up front alone
and I score the goals!"

"My dad bought me boots," Titch
said. But nobody listened to Titch.

Bungo kicked off, rolling the ball to Ravi.

"Pass back to me NOW!" Bungo roared, and Ravi did, even though he was better positioned.

Bungo went on a run, but his shot was saved by the goalie.

Then Dunky got
the ball. He passed
to Tony. Tony
trapped the ball and
looked
up ...
but Bungo was out
of position.
"Pass to me
NOW!" Bungo
bawled,
going red in the face.
Tony headed for
goal. He beat the
back *twice*, and
weaved in and out
with the ball.

15

"PASS! PASS! PASS!" screamed
Bungo, standing with his hands on
his hips. "YOU MUST PASS TO ME!"
Then Bungo ran over and crash-
tackled Tony. Tony fell down hurt.
Bungo took the ball and shot.

G·O·A·L!

"BUNGO'S TEAM!
BUNGO'S TEAM!"
shouted Bungo.
He took his shirt
off and waved it
round his head.

Me me me me!

"You're not supposed to tackle
your own team," Mrs Pearl told
Bungo.

"Sorry Ref. Stupid Tony wouldn't
pass," Bungo said, but he wasn't
sorry one bit.

"I'm the World-Cup King!" Bungo told Tony. "You *must* pass to me when I say so."

Tony limped off and little Titch came on as sub.

"Don't get in my way, or else!" Bungo warned Titch. "Our team has to be tough. Tinies like you won't win the World Cup for us."

Then Spain got on top.

Goal! Goal! Goal!

3–1 to Spain at half-time.

"The World-Cup King is going on all-out attack in this half," Bungo boasted.

He barged about and knocked all the little ones over. He still wouldn't pass to anyone else but...

The World-Cup King scored with
a rocket shot that whammed into
the back of the net.

"ME! ME! ME!" Bungo yelled.
"Somebody call Man United!"
Bungo tore off his shirt again and
ran to the fans.

"Put your shirt back on at once, Bungo," ordered Mrs Pearl.

"I'm going for my hat-trick!" yelled Bungo. "I'm KING OF THE CUP!"

"Be quiet, Bungo … or else," said Mrs Pearl. Then Bungo tripped someone up and Mrs Pearl gave Spain a free kick.

Goal!

Spain won the game 4–2.

"TEAM SCHEME for the next game!" Bungo told Ravi. "Your mate Tony is dropped for good because he's not a team player. Titch is out because he's so tiny. Cosmo will play. I'll bang in super-goals and we'll win the game."

"My new boots are brilliant," Titch told everyone. But no one was listening.

Mrs Scott was ref, and she blew the whistle.

"Pass to me!" Bungo yelled at Ravi, and he set off for goal.

BIFF! The World-Cup King was knocked flat-splatt by Cyrus, the sweeper.

"Don't do that again!" Bungo warned Cyrus.

"Oh yeah?" said Cyrus, and then he did it again.

Trinidad weren't like Spain. Cyrus was bigger than Bungo, and his team *all* passed to each other. Leroy saved lots of shots, because he was a really good goalie.

Then Cyrus moved up from the back, where he'd been marking Bungo. Bungo didn't tackle him. Bungo only tackled the tinies, and Cyrus got free and scored all their goals.

and another

Bungo started to kick everyone (except Cyrus). Mrs Scott told him to keep his cool or she'd give him a yellow card. Bungo went into a sulk.

Dunky scored
the only goal for
Bungo's Team.
Dunky got the ball in midfield …

and he beat Cyrus …
rushed in on the
goalie … and hit a
cracking right footer
into the top of the net.

G-O-A-L!

"You got lucky beating Cyrus,"
Bungo told Dunky. "Next time you
pass it to ME!" Trinidad Rovers won
5–1.

"There *must* be a team worse
than us!" groaned little Cosmo, but
nobody thought that there was.

Everyone thought that Tony
should play in the next game in
place of Cosmo, but Bungo picked
Titch instead. Ravi and Dunky
were cross, but they were too
scared of what Bungo might do to
say anything.

"I knew I'd get back in the
team!" little Titch said.

"TEAM SCHEME!" announced Bungo, and he turned to Titch. "You go in goal so Leroy can play in defence."

"Titch is too titchy to be goalie," Ravi objected.

"It doesn't matter," Bungo boasted. "I'll score bags of goals. Leroy will give me good passes."

"Wait and see," Titch said. "I bet I'll be the best goalie ever."

Titch did his best, but his best wasn't much. He let in two goals in four minutes.

Goal!

Goal!

"I'm going in goal. Titch is useless!" bawled the World-Cup King.

He chucked Titch out of goal, and went in himself.

Then the Peru striker got in an inswinging cross. Bungo went for the ball … and punched it into his own net. It was a *stupid* own goal!

Next Bungo let one in through his legs.

In Peru's next attack, Bungo kicked the striker. He should have got a red card but Mrs Scott let him stay on.

"Penalty kick to Peru!" she told everyone.

"You go in goal for the rest of the game, Ravi!" ordered Bungo.

"No fear!" said Ravi. That meant Leroy ended up back in goal.

He saved lots of shots and he only let in two goals, which was one goal less than Bungo.

Peru won 7–0!

"Tony should be in the team," Ravi said. "He's the best player we have!"

"I'm not having *your* mate Tony in *my* team!" said the World-Cup King. He brought Cosmo in.

"You're dropped!" Bungo told Titch.

Ravi kicked off, and Bungo burst
through, but some kid tripped the
World-Cup King.

Bungo went mad. The kid ran
away, and Bungo ran after him
shouting. The ref blew a big blast
on her whistle, yelling at Bungo
to stop.

Then Bungo
threw the ball at
the ref.

"That's it,
Bungo!" said
the ref.

The ref for the
match was Bungo's
mum. She showed
Bungo a yellow
card. Then she
yellow-carded
the kid who'd
tripped Bungo,
and gave
Bungo's Team a
penalty kick.

PEEP!

37

"I'll take it!" said the World-Cup
King, and he grabbed the ball from
his mum and put it on the spot.
Bungo blasted it over the bar.

Then Wales scored two goals.
Cosmo was hurt, and Bungo's
Team were down to four men.

"Bring Tony on as your sub,"
said Ravi, though he knew Bungo
wouldn't do it.

"I'm not bringing *him* on again,
ever!" Bungo said, and he called
Titch on instead.

"Here I come, Super-Sub!" yelled
Titch, but nobody listened to Titch.

Wales got two more goals straight after half-time, which made it 4–0.

Bungo was raging. He was yelling and bouncing about.

Then he flattened another tiny.

Bungo's mum blew a loud blast on her whistle. "Dangerous play!" she said, and she pulled out a RED card!

The World-Cup
King was sent off by
his mum! Bungo
tore off his shirt. He
started stamping and
shouting, but his mum
wouldn't let him back on.
Wales won 8–0.

"I'm not playing any more!"
yelled the World-Cup King.

"That's right,
Bungo," said Tony.
"Your mum sent
you off, so you're
suspended. That
means you miss the
last game."

This was how the World Cup
Table stood, before the final games.

	P	W	D	L	PTS
Wales	4	4	0	0	12
Trinidad Rovers	4	3	0	1	9
Peru	4	2	0	2	6
Spain	4	1	1	2	4
Brazil	4	0	1	3	1
Bungo's Team	4	0	0	4	0

"We are the worst team there is," said Cosmo, and he wouldn't play any more. That meant Titch had to be in and Tony could make his comeback, now Bungo was out of the team.

"You'll be all right now Bungo's gone," Ravi told Titch.

Thumbs up, Titch

"If we win this one we won't finish bottom!" Tony and Ravi told everyone. They had a Top Secret Plan for beating Brazil.

The Top Secret Plan was: *Titch as lone striker up front.*

"Titch as striker?" groaned Bungo.

"Small pitch, no offside, and Brazil have a nervy goalie," Ravi said. "Work it out for yourself, smartypants!"

"I bet I score trillions of goals!" boasted Titch.

BUNGO'S TEAM v BRAZIL

Bungo's Team kicked off without
the World-Cup King. Titch ran up
the field, and stood right in front of
the goalie. When the goalie moved,
Titch moved.

"Shove off, Titch. I can't see the ball!" yelled the goalie. "You can't stand in front of me. You're offside!"

"There *is* no offside in Mrs Pearl's five-a-side rules!" Tony told the goalie.

Mrs Pearl said that Tony was right.

Brazil went on the attack …

but Leroy was brilliant.
He saved again …

and again …

and AGAIN!

Tony and Ravi and Dunky all
hung back and tackled.

Then Leroy threw the ball to Tony. He was MILES out, but he shot. The ball headed straight for Titch, and the goalie.

"I can't see the ball!" yelled the goalie.

Titch jumped and muddled the goalie. The ball went past them both, and came off the post.

"You do that again and I'll get you!" the goalie yelled.

The next time he knocked Titch
over, trying to get to the ball.

The ref gave a free kick against
Titch for obstructing the goalie,
and she scolded the goalie for
banging into little Titch.

Half-time came, with no goals.

The goalie said he would clobber Titch, but Mrs Pearl heard him and blew her whistle.

"Touch him and you're off!" she warned the goalie.

Brazil were still trying to score lots of goals. *Everyone* shot … and Leroy saved the lot!

Then Dunky got the ball, and he kicked it upfield, which wasn't far. Tony ran past the full back and he shot … straight at Titch, and the goalie.

The goalie banged into Titch at the same time as the ball. The ball hit Titch on the knee ... and bounced into the net for a –

G·O·A·L !

Titch ran up the field punching
the air and shouting

"GOAL!"

Tony lifted him up in the air, then the whole team mobbed little Titch.

Titch for ever!

"I couldn't see!" said the goalie, but no one was listening. Bungo's Team were one up with two minutes to go.

Brazil went on all-out attack.

"Everyone back!" yelled Tony.

"Even me?" said Titch. "I might get another goal if I stay up front."

"You might not," said Tony. "Just stay back and get in the way!"

And the whole team fell back, defending.

Everyone tackled, even Titch.
Leroy was brilliant. He saved the
ball again … and again … and
again … and again.

The last one was a triple-save.
Leroy turned the ball onto the bar.

The ball bounced back and someone else shot. Leroy pushed it onto the post.

The ball bounced off the post, the striker lunged in and Leroy grabbed the ball off his foot.

Then the whistle blew for full time, and a 1–0 win, with the winning goal scored by Titch!

"We won," Tony and Ravi told Bungo. "That means we finished two points above Brazil, when you said we would lose without you and we'd finish last!"

"I SCORED THE WINNING GOAL!" yelled Titch.

And everyone said he was their
World-Cup Star Striker!

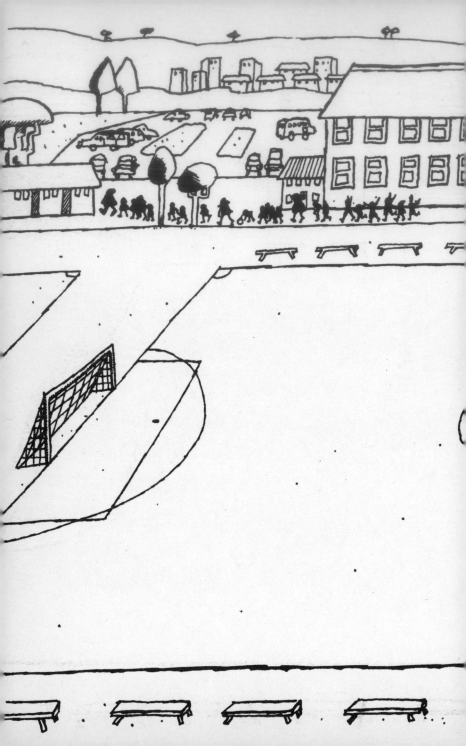

Sprinters

Fun Sprinters for you to enjoy!

Captain Abdul's Pirate School	Colin McNaughton
Care of Henry	Anne Fine
Cool as a Cucumber	Michael Morpurgo
Cup Final Kid	Martin Waddell
Ernie and the Fishface Gang	Martin Waddell
Fearless Fitzroy	Kathy Henderson
Fighting Dragons	Colin West
The Finger-eater	Dick King-Smith
The Haunting of Pip Parker	Anne Fine
Impossible Parents	Brian Patten
Jolly Roger	Colin McNaughton
Lady Long-legs	Jan Mark
Molly and the Beanstalk	Pippa Goodhart
Nag Club	Anne Fine
No Tights for George!	June Crebbin
Patrick's Perfect Pet	Annalena McAfee
Posh Watson	Gillian Cross
The Snow Maze	Jan Mark
Star Striker Titch	Martin Waddell
Taking the Cat's Way Home	Jan Mark
Tarquin the Wonder Horse	June Crebbin
Tricky Nelly's Birthday Treat	Berlie Doherty
The Vampire Across the Way	Dyan Sheldon